P9-BZV-698

The Museum *of* Everything

LYNNE RAE PERKINS

GREENWILLOW BOOKS, *An Imprint of HarperCollinsPublishers*

When the world gets too big
and too loud and too busy,
I like to look at little pieces
of it, one at a time.

I put them in a quiet place, like museums do.
Sometimes the quiet place is just in my mind. An
imaginary museum.

But I think I could make a real one.

Maybe it would be called the Museum of Things
I Wonder About. Because I have a lot of those.

I wonder about things like, can a rock in a puddle be
an island? And think about if the rock in the puddle
is on a boulder in a pond. And what if that pond is on
a small island in a lake? And what if that lake is on a
bigger island, out in the ocean?

It would be an island in a pond on an island in a
pond on an island in a pond on an island in a pond.

My museum will have a model of this.

I might make a whole Museum of Islands,
because there are so many different kinds.

And all different sizes. Some islands only
have room for one person at a time.

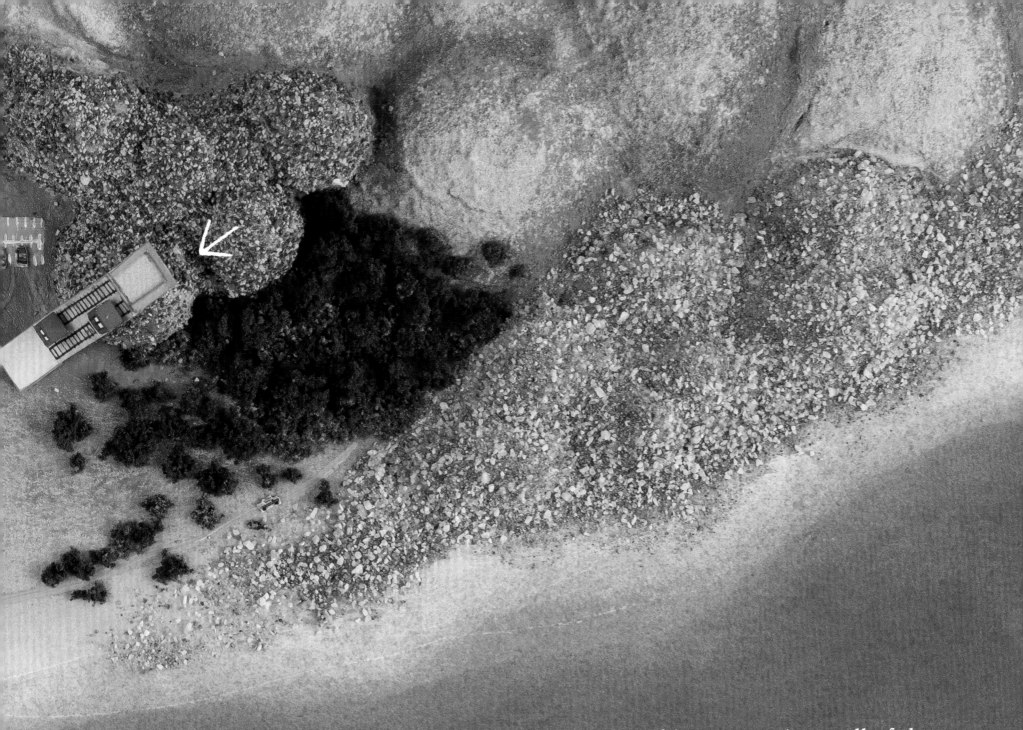

Other islands are so big, you can't see all of the edges, even from the top of a very high hill.

I wonder if anyone has ever made a skirt that looks like a bush in springtime, because I want to. I want to wear one.

There will be a whole roomful of bushskirts in my Museum of Bushes. Everyone can try them on, and twirl.

There will be real bushes, too. There will be wild bushes and tame ones, plain bushes and fancy ones.

Maybe even some experimental, science fiction-type bushes. I like them all.

There is a bush that, every time I see it, I think, that would be a good hiding place. For birds and little animals, but even for a person. I will have some of these bushes, for people to hide out in.

But maybe the hiding-place bush should be in a Museum of Hiding Places.

What if you walked right into a Museum of Hiding Places, and you didn't even know it? What if we're in one right now, and we can't even tell?

Look around . . . look in the shadows . . .

I might make a whole museum just of shadows.

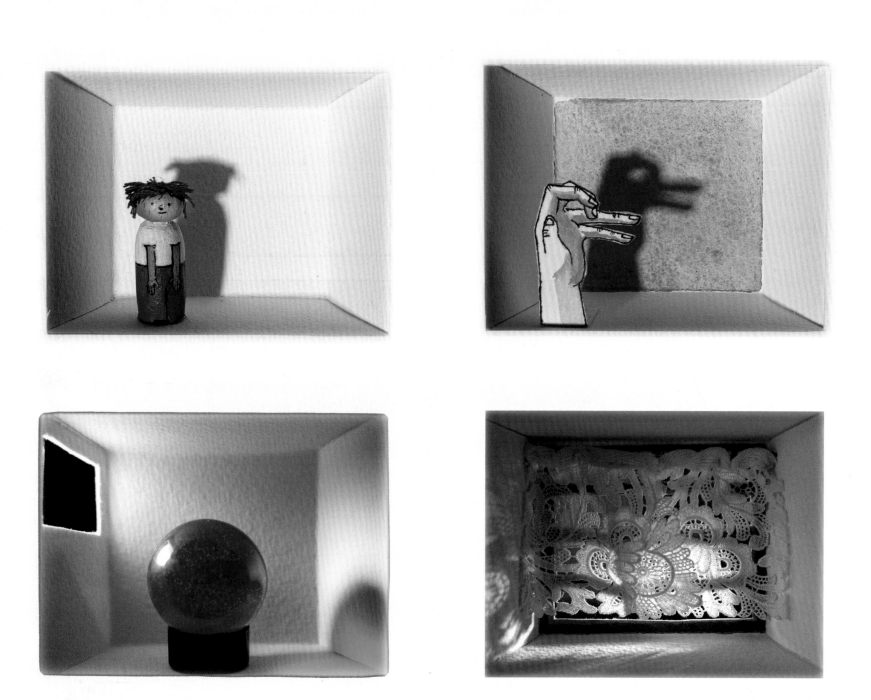

It will have all of the usual kinds.

All of the kinds you would expect.

But also some kinds you don't expect.

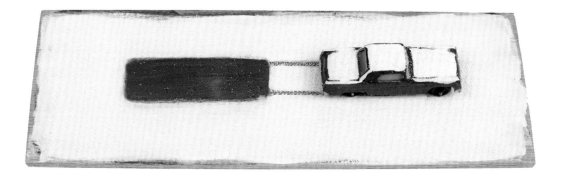

When snow falls on a car, and then the car drives away, the car shape that didn't get snowed on could be a kind of shadow.

Or when a leaf, warmed by sunlight, melts a perfect leaf-shaped hole in the snow. A shadow of melting.

A shadow could be made of blossoms
that fell from their tree overnight.

Or it could be made of autumn leaves.

There is a place between streetlights where
the shadow from behind you disappears, and
the shadow from in front of you hasn't started
yet. Is it a place with no shadows?

Or is it a place with 100 percent shadows?

The Sky Museum is already there. It's on a hilltop.
Or on the roof of a building. Or anywhere, really.
It's open all the time. It's different every day.
Usually there are birds, and sometimes airplanes.

On cloudy days, the sky reminds me of
the pages of a huge, giant book.
The first page might be woolly and gray, but if
you turn it over . . .

the other side of it is fluffy and sunlit.

There might be
a wispy page,
delicate like lace.

Then
a page of
the bluest
blue.

And then the pages of
the whole universe.
A bunch of them,
with stories of
the stars and
the planets.
And spaceships.

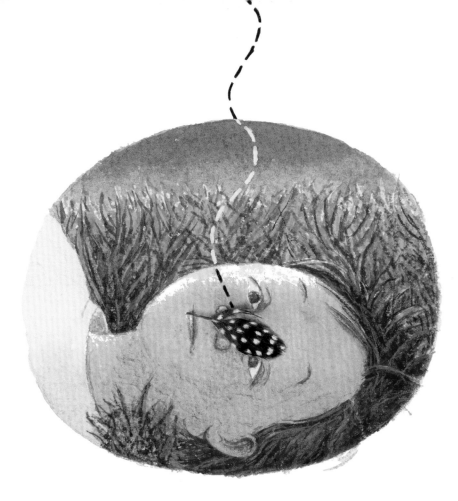

One day at the Sky Museum, a feather floated down and
landed on my nose: a free souvenir. I took it home and put it
on my windowsill between my very small island and a couple
of shadows and some other stuff that I have.

It's a real museum, a Museum of Little Things. I like to sit
and look at them, one at a time and all together.

And then I go back outside, where it's busy, and big, and
sometimes kind of noisy. Because sometimes I love that.

I walk right into the jumble. I see the little pieces of the world all fitting together, like the biggest puzzle ever.

Like the notes in a song.

Like the Museum of Everything.

If you like to be in a quiet place sometimes (even if it's only in your mind),
or if there is a lot that you wonder about,
or if you like to make things,
I made this book for you.

So many thanks to Michael Poehlman, our wonderful photographer!

The art in this book is made of watercolor on (Arches® 300lb cold press) watercolor paper, sometimes cut and/or folded, along with sand, stones, twigs, wood, moss, wool, foamcore board, fabric, embroidery thread, modeling clay, lights, two tiny clay figures made by Marcia Hovland, and many, many, many odds and ends. It was the most fun ever. More info at www.lynnerae.com.

Library of Congress Cataloging-in-Publication Data

Names: Perkins, Lynne Rae, author.
Title: The Museum of Everything / written and illustrated by Lynne Rae Perkins.
Description: First edition. | New York : Greenwillow Books, an Imprint of HarperCollins Publishers, [2021] | Audience: Ages 4–8. | Audience: Grades K–1. | Summary: When the world feels too big, loud, and busy, a young girl imagines a museum where she can organize little pieces of it and wonder about them.
Identifiers: LCCN 2020051381 | ISBN 9780062986306 (hardcover)
Subjects: CYAC: Museums—Fiction. | Imagination—Fiction.
Classification: LCC PZ7.P4313 Mus 2021 | DDC [E]—dc23 LC record available at https://lccn.loc.gov/2020051381

21 22 23 24 25 RTLO 10 9 8 7 6 5 4 3 2 1
First Edition
Greenwillow Books